BERRIES
for the
QUEEN
A Book about Patience

Janet Noonan and Jacquelyn Calvert
Illustrated by Scott Holladay

Chariot Books™
David C. Cook Publishing Co.

Chariot Books™ is an imprint of David C. Cook Publishing Co.
David C. Cook Publishing Co., Elgin, Illinois 60120
David C. Cook Publishing Co., Weston, Ontario
Nova Distribution Ltd., Newton Abbot, England

BERRIES FOR THE QUEEN
© 1993 by Janet Noonan and Jacquelyn Calvert for text and Scott Holladay for illustrations

Designed by Terry Julien
First Printing, 1993
Printed in the United States of America
97 96 95 94   5 4 3 2

Library of Congress Cataloging-in-Publication Data
Noonan, Janet, 1915-
Berries for the Queen / by Janet Noonan, Jacquelyn Calvert.
         p.   cm.
Summary: Angry and impatient in her craving for strawberries when they are out of season, the Queen finds herself being cruel to her subjects. Emphasizes that God is patient, kind, and slow to anger and that love does not insist on its own way.
ISBN 0-7814-0903-9
[1. Kings, queens, rulers, etc.—Fiction. 2. Strawberries—Fiction. 3. Christian life—Fiction.]
I. Calvert, Jacquelyn, 1943- . II. Title.
PZ7.N7398Be 1993
[E]—dc20   92-32336
                       CIP
                       AC

**W**hile strolling in
her garden one spring day,
the Queen made a discovery.

She spotted a bright red berry hiding beneath the soft green leaves of the strawberry plant.

It was the first, the very first one of the season.

The Queen clapped her hands in delight. "Oh," she exclaimed, "I would love a sweet strawberry tart right now."

Her mouth watered as she pictured a crisp tart piled high with the fresh rosy fruit. A mound of whipped cream swirled on top.

"I must have one," she sighed. She rang for her servant, James.

James," she commanded, "go to the kitchen and bring me a strawberry tart at once."

"Yes, Your Majesty," he replied, and he ran downstairs to the kitchen.

"Cook," commanded James, "the Queen desires a fresh strawberry tart at once."

"I'm sure I'm sorry, James," replied Cook, wiping her floury hands on her big white apron. "But there's not a single strawberry in the pantry."

James returned to the Queen, empty-handed.

"Begging your pardon, Ma'am," he said, bowing, "but the cook has no strawberries."

"That dolt," snapped the Queen. "Throw her in the dungeon. Go to the shop in the village and buy some strawberries."

"Yes, Your Majesty," James replied.

Quickly James jumped on his horse and rode off to the village greengrocer's shop. "Greengrocer," he demanded. "I need some fresh strawberries for a royal strawberry tart. The Queen is craving one right now."

"I'm sure I'm sorry to disappoint Her Highness," replied the greengrocer, "but there's not a single strawberry in the shop."

James returned to the Queen, empty-handed.

"Begging your pardon, Ma'am," he said, bowing, "but the greengrocer has no strawberries."

"What a total dolt," she cried, stamping her foot. "Throw him in the dungeon. I want strawberries right now! Go to the farm and pick some."

"Yes, Your Majesty," James replied.

So James mounted his horse again and rode off to the farm. He found the farmer weeding carrots in the kitchen garden.

"Biggins," he called, jumping off his horse. "Please pick me some strawberries right now. Her Highness is demanding a fresh strawberry tart at once."

"I'm very sorry, I'm sure, James," replied the farmer, pulling off his muddy gloves, "but I have no strawberries. Strawberries won't be ripe until later this spring."

James returned to the Queen, empty-handed.

"Begging your pardon, Ma'am," he said, bowing, "but the farmer has no strawberries. He says strawberries are not in season."

"Liar!" shouted the Queen. "I found one this morning in my own garden. Throw him in the dungeon. Go search the kingdom for strawberries."

"Yes, Your Majesty," James replied.

So James rode his trusty horse from one end of the kingdom to the other.

Soon he returned to the Queen, empty-handed.

"Your Majesty," he said, bowing, "I have searched the kingdom. There are no strawberries."

"You double, doubly dolt," she screamed in a rage, and called the castle guards.

"Throw this man in the dungeon," she commanded.

Quickly they dragged poor James to the dungeon.

Still craving a strawberry tart, the Queen plucked the one luscious berry from its nest of green leaves.

"Well," she pouted, "if I can't have a tart, I will at least have strawberries and cream."

So she rang for her maid, Dora.

"Bring me a crystal bowl, a silver spoon, and a jug of rich cream," the Queen ordered.

"Yes, Your Majesty," Dora replied, curtsying.

Dora skipped down to the kitchen. "Where is Cook?" she asked Audrey, the scullery maid.

"Haven't you heard?" replied Audrey. "Cook is in the dungeon!"

"Oh, la!" exclaimed Dora, and ran upstairs to the parlor, empty-handed.

"Begging your pardon, Ma'am, but the cook is in the dungeon and the pantry is locked."

"You dunce," cried the Queen. "Go to the shop in the village and buy some cream."

"Yes, Your Majesty," Dora replied, curtsying.

Dora trudged the long, hot, dusty road down to the shop in the village. When she got there, she found a big lock on the door and the greengrocer's wife sitting on a three-legged stool, weeping.

"Why isn't the shop open?" demanded Dora. "Call your husband to come open up quickly. I need some thick cream for the Queen."

"Haven't you heard, girl?" snapped the greengrocer's wife. "My poor husband is in the dungeon."

"Oh, la!" exclaimed Dora, and limped back to the castle on her blistered feet, empty-handed.

Begging your pardon, Ma'am, but the greengrocer is in the dungeon and the shop is locked."

"You dense dunce," shouted the Queen, stamping her foot. "Go to the farm and get some cream from the cow."

"Yes, Your Majesty," Dora replied, curtsying.

As Dora ran down the lane to the farm, she passed the cows grazing in the meadow. Knocking at the farmhouse door, she called, "Mrs. Biggins, give me some cream right away. The Queen is demanding cream for her strawberry."

"Oh, Dora," sobbed the farmer's wife, throwing her arms around the maid. "Haven't you heard? Biggins is in the dungeon. We have no cream because there is no one to drive the cows into the barn for milking," she wailed. "Oh, what is to become of us?"

Dora returned to the castle, empty-handed.

"Begging your pardon, Ma'am, but the farmer is in the dungeon and the cows are in the meadow."

"You double dense dunce," screamed the Queen. "Search the kingdom for some cream."

"Yes, Your Majesty," Dora said, curtsying.

Obediently, Dora ran through the crooked streets of the kingdom, knocking on every cottage door, demanding cream for the Queen.

Soon she came back, empty-handed, and fell to her knees, trembling.

"Your Majesty," she stammered, "your subjects are hoarding their cream."

"And why, may I ask?" demanded the angry Queen.

"They fear they will starve," wept Dora. "They say their pantries will soon be empty because the greengrocer and the farmer are in the dungeon."

"Fiddlesticks!" replied the Queen.

"They say," Dora sobbed, "that you are an angry and cruel Queen."

"You double, doubly dense dunce!" the Queen sputtered with rage. "I'll call the castle guards and have you thrown—"

She stopped and looked at Dora, quaking before her.

T hey said they will starve?"

"Yes, Your Majesty."

"They said their pantries will soon be empty?"

"Yes, Your Majesty."

"They said I am angry and cruel?"

"Yes, Your Majesty."

"Dear me," said Her Majesty. *"I am a dunce! I am a double, dense dunce! I didn't know I was being angry and cruel just because I craved a strawberry tart."*

The Queen called the castle guards and ordered them to free the prisoners in the dungeon.

"When strawberries are in season," she proclaimed, "I will have a strawberry tart festival for all my subjects. And to remind me not to be angry and cruel, we will have a festival every year, as long as I am Queen."

And all her subjects cheered their kind Queen.

The Queen learned that when she became angry and impatient, she behaved cruelly towards her subjects; but she loved her subjects and didn't want to hurt them. She determined to be patient in the future.

God is patient and kind, and slow to anger. He loves us very much. Can you think of ways God has been patient and loving to you?

Love is patient and kind; love is not jealous or boastful; it is not arrogant or rude. Love does not insist on its own way.
1 Corinthians 13:4, 5 (RSV)